THE BRIDE OF THE ISLES

BY

JAMES ROBINSON PLANCHE

British Library Cataloguing-in-Publication Data
A catalogue record for this book is available from
the British Library

Contents

JAMES ROBINSON PLANCHÉ

James Robinson Planché was born in Piccadilly, London in 1796. He became interested in theatre at an early age, joining an amateur company and producing his first play, *Amoroso, King of Little Britain*, in 1818. The success of this production led him to take up playwriting full-time, and he produced a new work almost yearly, going on to write a total of 176 plays. Arguably the most successful of these was *The Island of Jewels* (1849). Planché was also a highly successful costume designer – his *History of British Costume* (1834) and *A Cyclopaedia of Costume: Or, Dictionary of Dress* (1876-1879) are still standard reference texts – and an early campaigner for dramatic copywriting laws. In 1869, at the request of the War Office, Planché arranged the collection of armour at the Tower of London in chronological order. He died in Chelsea in 1880.

*   *   *

There is a popular superstition *still extant* in the southern isles of Scotland, but not with the force as it was a century since, that the souls of persons, whose actions in the mortal state were so wickedly attrocious as to deny all possibility of happiness in that of the next;

were doomed to everlasting perdition, but had the power given them by infernal spirits to be for awhile the scourge of the living.

This was done by allowing the wicked spirit to enter the body of another person at the moment their own soul had winged its flight from earth; the corpse was thus reanimated – the same look, the same voice, the same expression of countenance, with physical powers to eat and drink, and partake of human enjoyments, but with the most wicked propensities, and in this state they were called Vampires. This second existence, as it may not improperly be termed, is held on a tenure of the most horrid and diobolical nature. Every *All-Hallow E'en*, he must wed a lovely virgin, and slay her, which done, he is to catch her warm blood and drink it, and from this draught he is renovated for *another* year, and free to take *another* shape, and pursue his Satannic course; but if he failed in procuring a wife at the appointed time, or had not opportunity to make the sacrifice before the moon set, the Vampire *was no more* – he did not turn into a skeleton, but literally vanished into air and nothingness.

One of these demoniac sprites, Oscar Montcalm, of infamous notoriety in the Scotch annals of crime and murder, (who was decapitated by the hands of the common executioner), was a most successful Vampire, and many were the poor unfortunate maidens who had been sacrificed to support his supernatural career, roving from place to place, and every year changing his shape as opportunity presented itself, but always choosing to enter the corpse of some man of rank and power, as by that means his voracious appetite for luxury was gratified.

Oscar Montcalm had seen, and distantly adored in his mortal state, the superior beauty of the Lady Margaret, daughter of the Baron of the Isles, the good Lord Ronald; but, such was his situation, he had not dared to address her; however, he did not forget her in his Vampire state, but marked her out for one of his victims, in revenge for the scorn with which he had been treated by her father.

Lady Margaret, though lovely and well proportioned, entered her twentieth year unmarried, nor had she ever been addressed by a suitor whom she could regard with the least partiality, and with much anxiety she sought to know whether she should ever enter into wedlock, and what sort of person her future lord would be. With credulity pardonable to the times in which she lived, and the narrow education then given to females, even of rank, she consulted Sage Seer and Witch, as to this important event; but it is not to be wondered at that she met with many contradictions, every one telling a different tale. At length urged on by the irresistible desire to pry into futurity, she repaired with her two maidens, Effie and Constance, to the CAVE of FINGAL, where, cutting off a lock of her hair, and joining it to a ring from her finger, she cast it into the well, according to the directions she had received from Merna, the Hag of the mountains, who had instructed the fair one as to this expedition.

No sooner was the ring flung into well than a dreadful storm arose; the torches, which the attendant maidens had borne, were extinguished, and the immense cave was in utter darkness: loud and dreadful was the thunder, accompanied by a horrid confusion of sounds, which beggars description.

Margaret and her companions sunk on their knees; but they were too stupified with horror: to pray, or to endeavour to retrace their way out of this den of horrors. Of a sudden, the cave was brilliantly illuminated. But with no visible means of light, for there were neither torch, lamp, or candle. Solemn music was heard, slow and awfully grand, and in a few minutes two figures appeared, one heavy morose in countenance, and clad in dark robes, who announced herself as Uno, the spirit of the storm, and touching a sable curtain, discovered to the view of Margaret the figure of a noble young warrior, Ruthven, earl of Marsden, who had accompanied her father to the wars. Again the storm resounded, the curtain closed, and the cave resumed its darkness; but this was only transient – the brilliant light returned – Una was gone, and the light figure, dressed in transparent robes, sprinkled over with spangles remained. With her wand she pulled aside the curtain, and a young man of interesting appearance was visible, but his person was a stranger to the fair one. Ariel, the spirit of the Air, then waved her hand to the entrance of the cave, as a signal for them to depart, and bowing low, they withdrew, amid strains of heart thrilling harmony, rejoiced to find themselves once more in an open space, and they happily returned in safety to the baron's castle. The Lady Margaret was well pleased with what she had seen, as promising her two husbands, though she was somewhat puzzled by calling to mind a couplet that Ariel had repeated three or four times, while the curtain remained undrawn.

> 'But once, fair maid, will you be wed,
> 'You'll know no second bridal bed.'

What could this mean? Surely she would never stoop to illicit desires or intrigue? She thought she knew her own heart too well.

The Vampire had seen into the designs of Margaret to visit the Cave of Fingal, and he sought out Ariel and Uno, to whom, by virtue of his supernatural rights, he had easy access. The spirit of the air would not befriend him, but the spirit of the storm assisted him to pry into futurity; and to suit his views, she presented the figure of Ruthven, earl of Marsden. In the mean time, Marsden had the good fortune to save Lord Ronald's life in the battle, and the wars being ended, or at least suspended for a time, he invited the gallant youth home with him to his castle, to pass a few months amid the social rites of hospitality and the pleasures of the chase.

The Lady Margaret received her father with dutiful affection, and gratitude to providence for his safe return, and she beheld young Marsden with secret delight; but when informed that he had preserved the baron from overpowering enemies, her gratitude knew no bounds, and she looked so beautiful and engaging, while returning her thankful effusions for the service he had rendered her father, that the earl could not resist the impulse, and from that hour became deeply enamoured of the lovely fair one.

Marsden's rank and birth were unexceptionable but his fortune was very inadequate to support a title, which made him (added to the love of military glory) enter into the profession of arms, of which he was an ornament.

Margaret was an only child, and her father abounding in wealth and honours; it might therefore be presumed that an ambition might lead him to form very exalted views for the aggrandizement of his heiress; and so he had, but perceiving how high his preserver stood in the good graces of his darling child, and that the passion was becoming mutual, he resolved not to give any interruption to their happiness, but if Marsden could win Margaret to let him have her, as a rich reward for the service he had performed amid the clang of arms.

Parties were daily formed by the baron for the chace, hawking, or fishing, while the evening was given to the festive dance, or the minstrels tuned their harps in the great hall, and sang the deeds of scottish chiefs, long since departed, amongst whom the heroic Wallace was not forgot.

The loves of Ruthven and Lady Margaret were now generally known throughout the islands and congratulations poured in from every quarter.

A day was fixed for the nuptials, and magnificent preparations were made at the castle for the celebration of the ceremony, when the sudden and severe illness of the baron caused a delay. He wished them not to defer their marriage on his account; but the young people, in this instance, would not obey him, declaring their joys would be incomplete without his revered presence.

The baron blessed them for this instance of love and filial duty, but he still felt a strong desire to have the marriage concluded.

The baron was scarce recovered, when he and Ruthven were summoned to the field of battle, a war having broke out in Flanders, and the marriage was deferred till their return; and taking a most affectionate leave of the Lady Margaret, the father and lover left the castle, and the fair one in the charge of old Alexander, the faithful steward, with many commands and cautions respecting the edifice and the Lady, whom they both regarded as a gem of inestimable value, with whom they were loath to part, but imperious duty and the calls of honour allowed no alternative.

Robert, the old Steward's son, attended the baron abroad; and Marsden took his own servant the faithful Gilbert. They were successful in several skirmishes with the enemy, but in the final engagement Ruthven lost his life, dying in the arms of the Lord of the Isles, who mourned over him as for a beloved son, and he ordered Robert and Gilbert, who were on the spot, to convey the body to a place beyond the carnage, that when the battle was over he might see it, (if he himself survived,) and have the valued remains interred in a manner that became an earl and a soldier, dying in defending his country's cause.

The battle ended, for the glory and success of Great Britain, and the good Baron of the Isles was unhurt, so was Robert, but Gilbert was amongst the slain.

Lord Ronald, fatigued with the sharp action of the day, in which he had borne his part with a vigour surprising to his time of life, for his head was now silvered over with the honourable badge of age, repaired to his tent to take some refreshment and an hour's rest on his couch, to invigorate his frame. The couch eased his weary limbs, but his eyes closed not, and all his thoughts were on Ruthven, and the distress the sad news would give to his dear child. He arose, and with trembling fingers penned a letter to her, describing the melancholy event, and exhorting her, for the sake of her father, to support this trial with resignation and patience, and bow to the dispensations of Providence, who orders all things eventually for the best, however severe and distressing they seem at the time. He ended his letter by observing that he should return to the castle of the Isles without delay, being anxious to fold her in his arms, and that he should bring the corpse of the brave Marsden to his native land.

The letter being sent off expressly by one of his retainers, the baron ordered some soldiers to attend with a bier, and taking Robert for their guide they went to fetch the body of Ruthven, and in the mean time he had a small tent erected for its reception, surmounted by a sable flag.

But this posthumous attention of the good baron was all in vain, for after a long absence, Robert and the soldiers returned, with the unwelcome news that the body of the gallant Scot was not to be found, but the spot where it had been deposited by the servants was still marked with the blood that had flowed from his gaping wounds and it was presumed that the enemy had found the corpse, and had conveyed it away to some obscure hole out of revenge for the slaughter he had dealt among their leaders before his fall. This event added materially to Ronald's regret and sorrow, for the natives of the Isles of Escotia held a traditional superstition, that while the body lay unburied the spirit wandered denied of rest. He offered rewards for the body without success, and was at length obliged, though with much reluctance, to drop the affair.

The baron was obliged to pay his duty in England to his sovereign before he repaired to the Isles. Unexpected events detained him two months at the British court, but he at last effected his departure to his long wished for home.

A courier made known his approach, and Lady Margaret, attended by the whole household, dressed in their best array, came forth to meet him, headed by the aged minstrel, and they received their lord with joyous shouts and lively strains, about half a mile from the gates of the castle.

Lord Ronald, as the carriage descended a steep hill that led into the valley, had a full view of the party approaching to meet him, and his heart felt elate at the compliment. He could discern his daughter; but how came it she was not in sables? Surely Ruthven, her betrothed lover, deserved that mark of respect to his memory! But he could observe that she was gaily dressed, and her high plume of feathers waving in the light breeze that adulated the air. The baron cast a look on his own deep mourning, and sighed; he was not pleased – but worse and worse. As he gained a nearer view, he perceived that his daughter was handed along, most familiarly by a knight. I had hoped, said he to himself, that Margaret would have rose superior to the inconstancy and caprice attributed to her sex. Can it be possible, that she has so soon forgot the valiant accomplished Ruthven! Oh, woman! woman! are ye all alike? As the vehicle entered the valley, Ronald quitted it, to receive the welcome of his child and retainers.

Powers of astonishment! was it, or was it not, illusion? By what miracle did he behold Ruthven, earl of Marsden, standing before him, and Lady Margaret hanging with chaste expressions of delight on his arm; there was a scar on his forehead, and he was much paler than before the battle, but no other alteration was visible. As for Robert, he stood aghast, his hair bristled up and his joints trembled, and altogether would have served as a good model of horror to a painter or statuary.

Ruthven stretched forth his hand – 'You seem astonished, my good lord,' said he, 'to find me here before you, or, indeed to find me here at all. I was discovered by some peasants returning from their daily labour, nearly covered with fern and leaves, ['Yes' said Robert, 'that was Gilbert's work and mine.'] by means of a little dog, who had scented out my body from its purposed concealment. They were very poor, and my clothes and decorations were a strong temptation, to which they yielded, they agreed to strip me, sell the clothes, and divide the spoil. While they were thus occupied, they perceived signs of life, and their humanity prevailed over every other consideration, I was conveyed to one of their cottages, and well attended. The man had a wonderful skill in herbs and simples, therefore my cure was rapid, but previous to my leaving them, I well rewarded every one who had been instrumental in my preservation and freely forgave the intended plunder they had confessed to me, as it was the means directed by fate to prolong my existence, and restore me to my angelic Margaret.

'When I recovered, I found the British forces had quitted Flanders, but I could not learn which direction my friend the baron (you my dear lord) had taken; so I hastened to Scotland with all the speed my situation would admit of, and we were retarded at sea by adverse winds. I found my dear betrothed, and her fair damsels, in deep mourning for my supposed loss; but I soon changed her tears for smiles, and her sables for gayer vestments: but at first her surprise, like yours, Lord Ronald, was too great to admit of utterance, but in time we became composed and grateful, and we agreed not to inform you of my existence, but astonish you on your arrival.'

The baron greeted his young friend most warmly and testified his hope that no more ill-omened events would disappoint the nuptials of the brave earl and Margaret, whom he tenderly clasped to his bosom, and kissing each cheek, remarked that she was the living image of his dear departed wife. He then turned to the old harper, and bidding him strike up a lively strain, proceeded to the castle, where all was joy and festivity; again resounded the song, and again the damsels, with their swains shewed off their best reels *a-la Caledonia*.

In the old steward's room a plenteous board was spread, for the upper servants and retainers of the hospitable Lord of the isles, who ordered flowing bowls and well replenished horns to the health of Ruthven and Margaret.

Some of the party were remarking on the wonderful preservation of Marsden's earl by the Flemish peasants, instead of plundering and leaving him to perish, as many would have done to an almost expiring enemy.

'*Almost expiring!*' said Robert, whose cheeks had not yet recovered their usual hue since the meeting in the valley with Ruthven.

'*Almost Expiring!*' he repeated; 'I am certain the body of the earl was dead – aye, as dead as my great grandsire – when I and Gilbert carried him from the field of battle; and when we left him under the fern he was as cold as ice, and the blood from his wounds coagulated – No, no, he never came to life again; this Ruthven you have here must be a Vampire.'

'*A Vampire! a Vampire!*' resounded from all the company, with loud shouts of laughter at poor Robert's simplicity. 'Perhaps you are a *Vampire*,' said his sweetheart, Effie, joining in the mirth, 'so I shall take care how I trust myself in your power.'

Robert did not reply, and all the rest of the night he had to stand the bantering jests of his companions.

But Robert was right; Marsden's earl died on the field of battle, and the moment the servants quitted the corpse, the Vampire, wicked Montcalm, whose relics lay smouldering beneath a stone in Fingal's cave, watching the moment, took possession, and reanimated the body; the wounds instantly healed, but the face wore a pallid hue, the invariable case with the Vampires, their blood not flowing, in that free circulation which belong to real mortals.

The story told by the Vampire was a fabrication, respecting the peasants, to impose on Lord Ronald and the Lady Margaret as to the appearance of the supposed Ruthven, and he well succeeded.

On previously consulting the Spirit of the Storm, the Vampire had discovered that Margaret would be courted by Ruthven, earl of Marsden; he also discovered, in his peep into futurity, that the young hero would be slain in battle, and this seemed to him a glorious opportunity to obtain possession of the lovely Margaret, and make her his victim, renovate his Vampireship, and go on in the most diabolical career, hurling destruction on the human race, and drawing them into crime after crime, till they sunk into the gulph of eternal infamy.

It now wanted a month to All Hallow E'en and it so chanced, that in that year the next coming moon would set on that very eve from its full orbit. The Vampire repaired to the cave of Fingal, and by magic means, which he well knew how to put in execution, he raised up some infernal spirits, whom he asked for orders. They told him they would consult their ruler Beelzebub, and he was to come on the third eve from thence for an answer.

This, then, was the decree – he must wed a virgin, destroy her, and drink her blood, before the setting of the moon on All Hallow E'en, or terminate into mere non-entity; and if the maid was unchaste, the charm was dissolved. If he succeeded he was to quit the form of earl Marsden and get egress into some other corpse to give it animation.

The supposed death of Ruthven had caused Margaret to imbibe the idea that the two figures she had seen in Fingal's cave, and Ariel's couplet prophetic but of one marriage, now made out by his fall, he being only a betrothed lover, and the stranger knight she regarded as her future spouse; but the return of the earl again puzzled her, and she knew not what to think, but at length resolved on another visit to the mystic cavern. Possibly ashamed of confessing this weakness to her maidens, or, what is more probable, conscious that from the terrors they had experienced in attending her there, she could not persuade them to go a second time, she went alone, and soon after midnight, when all the castle was hushed in sound repose, save the Vampire, who beheld from the lofty casement, the temporary flight of the enterprising Margaret. How did he thirst for her blood – how willingly would he have immolated the lovely maid that moment, and paid the infernal tribute, but for one clause that interposed and saved her from his fangs. This was the necessity of his being first legally married, in all due form, to the intended victim. He regarded her with a diabolical and malicious scowl, while, by as bright a star light as ever illumined the heavens, he saw her tripping through the park's wide avenues of stately firs. He wondered where she was going, and felt apprehensive that some event was in agitation that might deprive him of his bride. The Vampire had just concluded to follow her, when a heaviness, he could neither resist or shake off, overpowered him and sealed his eyes in a deep sleep.

Margaret, in much perturbation and a beating heart, gained the way to the cave; but the interior was so dark that she was obliged to grope on her hands and knees to the magic well, and cast in the accustomed charm. The thunder rolled, and the storm commenced, but with not one quarter of the violence as on her preceding visit. The music followed in an harmonious strain, and the spirits of the storm and air soon stood before her. The beauty, the innocence, of the noble maid, her virtues and her benevolence, had interested these mystical beings in her behalf – yes, even the stern and oft obdurate Una felt for Margaret, and wished to save her. They could not alter the decree of fate, nor had they power over the Vampires; the only thing that remained was to warn the inquirer, if possible, of her danger. For this purpose, they unfolded the curtain, and presented to her view, the real Ruthven on the field of battle, bleeding and a corpse. She heard his last sigh, saw his last convulsive motion; – *a grizzly fleshless skeleton stood by his side, and at that moment entered his corpse, which sprung up reanimated.* Margaret knew well the traditional tales of the Vampires, and shudderd as she beheld one before her; for what could be more plain? No further vision was shewn her – she was warned from the cave, and the fair one returned to the castle, dejected and spiritless. What did this mean? Ruthven, her adored Ruthven, could be no Vampire – impossible – so accomplished, so clever, superior in most things to others of his rank. – She past the intervening hours in a very restless state, till they met at their morning repast in the small saloon. The Vampire handed her to a chair; she remembered the scene in the cave, and shrank back with a feeling of disgust; but this was not lasting; the labours of the spirit of the storm and the air had not their intended effect; like advice given to young maidens that accords not with the inclination, it sank before the fascination of the object beloved, and she regarded what had been shewn her as wayward spite in Una and Ariel; so ready are we to twist circumstances to act in conformity with our own inclination.

The dews of night, the chilling breeze, the damp of the magic cave of Fingal, joined to the fatigue and agitation of the noble maiden, caused a fever which confined her to her chamber several days, and again delayed the marriage. The Vampire grew impatient, and before the Lady Margaret was scarce convalescent, he began to press for the nuptial ceremony, with what the good baron thought indecorous haste, though he made all possible allowance for repeated disappointments and youthful passions.

Robert, much better read than the warrior, his master, in the traditional tales of his country, and its popular superstitions, had not yet got the better of his shock at the re-appearance of Ruthven in his native valley, when he felt convinced that marsden's earl died of his wounds on the field of battle at Flanders. 'Aye, by the holy rood, he did,' would the youth often mutter to himself – 'May I never live to be married to my gentle Effie, and it wants but three days and three nights to that happy morn, if I did not see Ruthven's eye-strings crack, and heart's veins burst asunder: this is a Vampire, and this is the moon when those foul fiends pay their tribute, and now he is all impatience to wed my young mistress, forsooth – Yes, yes, 'tis plain enough: but what is the use of saying any thing about it, my father and all the servants laugh at me; even my intended turns into ridicule, any thing I advance on that subject, and calls me Robert, the Vampire hunter: but I will not be deterred from doing my duty like an honest servant, let them jeer as they will. I am resolved to tell the baron all that I know, that is, all I think of his guest, and then he may please himself, and come what will, my conscience will be clear.'

Robert had courage to face a cannon, and never turned his back on the bravest foe, but he felt daunted at the disclosure he meant to make to Lord Ronald; the subject was awkward, and the Vampire (if Vampire he was) might take a summary revenge on him for his interference. Yet his resolution was not shaken, and seeking the cellar-man he procured a glass of cordial and a horn of ale to revive his spirits, and then, finding himself what he called his own man again, he sought the baron, whom he happened to find a one and taking his evening walk in the grounds, while Margaret and her lover were sitting at their music.

Robert told his tale with much hesitation and faultering, but the baron heard him with more patience than he expected, and made him recount every particular of his suspicions. ' 'Tis strange! 'Tis marvellous strange!' replied the good Lord Ronald; 'for I have seen many persons from Flanders, and yet they never heard of the earl of Marsden being saved by the peasants: one would have thought such news would have spread like wildfire.'

'Neither does he go to mass or prayer,' observed Robert, 'as a christian warrior ought to do; nor does he take salt on his trencher.* And All-Hallow-E'en is fast approaching,' continued Robert: 'this is the fatal moon, and my young mistress –'

'Shall never be his,' exclaimed the baron 'till the moon sets, and the night, so tragic and pregnant of evil to many a spotless maid, is gone by; then if Ruthven is Marsden's true earl, he may have my Margaret. She shall then be his, and I will turn all my fish-ponds into bowls for whiskey punch, and the great fountain in the fore court shall flow with ale till not a Scot around can stand upon his legs, or he is no well-wisher to me or mine; but if he is an infernal Vampire, his reign will be

* This remark of Robert's was another popular Superstition of the Isles.

over. Faith, by St. Andrew, I know not what to think, but I have had fearful dreams, portentous of evil to my ancient house.'

The baron dismissed Robert with a present, and many encomiums on his fidelity and zeal for him and the Lady Margaret. 'My father,' said the honest fellow, 'has lived with you from youth to age: I was born within these walls, and my deceased mother suckled your amiable heiress; treachery in me would be double guilt: No, I would die to serve the house of Ronald!'

When the baron entered his daughter's appartment, a groupe met his eyes, very ill calculated to give him pleasure in his present frame of mind full of supernatural ideas, and teeming with dread suspicions; Margaret had changed her robes of plaid silk for virgin white, her neck chain, bracelets, and other ornaments of filagree silver, most exquisitely wrought. Ruthven was also dressed with elegance. The fair one's attendants were also in their best. The steward and the physician of the household were present, and the chaplain stood with the sacred book in his hand.

'We were waiting for you, my dear Lord Baron,' said the Vampire, Ruthven; 'I have persuaded my lovely betrothed to be mine this very evening. We have been so very unfortunate, that I dread further delay, and think every hour teeming with evil till she is mine irrevocably.'

'You have no rival,' answered the baron, much alarmed and piqued: 'you are secure in Margaret's love and my consent. My friends and tenants will ill brook such privacy; they have been accustomed to see the daughters of the Lord of the Isles wedded in public pomp and magnificence, and to share in the festive and abundant hospitalities. – No, by the shades of my ancestors, I will have no such doings.'

Ruthven pleaded hard, but the baron heeded not his arguments or eloquence, for the more he seemed bent on espousing Margaret then, the old lord thought more on Robert's report and his own suspicions. Margaret, infatuated by the spell that cast an illusion over her senses, seemed to forget her proper dignity and the delicate decorum of her sex, and joined in the solicitations of her lover. 'My dear father,' said the beauteous maiden, 'Ruthven and myself are in unison with each other's sentiments: we seek not in pomp and glare for happiness; we place our prospects of future bliss in elegant retirement and domestic pleasures. Allow us to be now united, I entreat you, and you can afterwards treat your neighbours, retainers, and servants, as plenteously as you like, but I shrink from the idea of a public marriage.'

Ruthven took the hand of his betrothed, which she presented to him with the most endearing smiles, while her eyes were modestly bent down and her cheeks covered with roseate blushes, and never did Lady Margaret look so irresistibly captivating as at that moment.

The baron, while she was speaking, trembled with emotion – Not for a single hour, said he, mentally, would I defer their happiness on account of bridal pomp, if I thought all was right; but I will not risk the sacrificing so much loveliness, and that my only child, the image of my lost Cassandra, to a Vampire; but he did not like to disclose the suspicions he had imbibed, for if they were founded in error, how grossly ridiculous would he appear, and he resolved to delay the nuptials, and stay the test of the moon. He therefore said, 'It is my pleasure to give a full month to splendid preparation, 'tis but a short delay, and let me have the satisfaction to have the nuptials as I would wish them to be, in honour of Marsden's earl and Ronald's daughter.'

The baron observed the lover give a start at the words 'a full month,' and his eyes shot forth a most malicious glance. He still held Margaret's hand. 'Nonsense! my good friend,' said he, – 'this is not fair, from one warrior to another – Chaplain, begin the ceremony.'

The enraged baron flung off his guard, snatched the book from the hands of the priest, and bade Margaret retire with her maidens to another room, accusing Ruthven of being a Vampire.

This was strongly resented by the accused, and, indeed, every one took his part, and laughed at the suggestion. This raised his passion so high that he was declared by the physician to be insane, and they coercively conveyed him to his chamber, and barred him in, where he was on the point of becoming frantic indeed, from the thoughts that the marriage might now take place in spite of his injunctions, for he was more convinced than ever of Ruthven being a supernatural imposter, or he would never have acted so uncourteous to a knight in his own castle.

Robert having heard from his father, the old steward, of the interruption of the marriage, through the baron's mania, in thinking the Earl of Marsden a Vampire, and his lord's confinement in the western turret, observed that he supposed the nuptials then were all off – His parent answered no, that the young people were not forced to obey such whims; that Lady Margaret was retired for an hour to regain her composure, and the chaplain would then perform the ceremony. 'And who is to be the bride's father?' said Robert. 'I am to have that honour,' replied the steward. – 'And much good may it do you,' said the son; 'but if I was you, I'd cater better for the noble lady Margaret than to give her to an evil spirit' – 'Go to, for an ungracious bird,' exclaimed Alexander; 'you are as mad as your master; poor Effie will have but a crazy husband at the best of it.' 'Better a crazy one, than a blood thirsty Vampire, father,' observed Robert, who quitted the room, vexed at the loud peal of laughter, which was now set up against him.

Robert went out into the park, but returned privately into the castle by a bye path and a private door, of which he had a key, having procured it some time before he went to the wars, for he was then a rakish youth, and loved to steal out to the village dance or festival, after he was supposed to retire to rest for the night; but now, he was contracted to the languishing blue-eyed Effie he was reformed, and voluntarily relinquished all such stolen delights. The key was now regarded by him as a treasure. 'It helped me,' said he to himself, to sow my wild oats; 'it shall now aid me to perform a more laudable purpose. Little did I think to see the good Baron of the Isles a captive in his own castle; and for what, but that he is in too much possession of his senses to sacrifice his lovely virgin daughter to a Vampire, for such, by the holy rood, is this fine Earl of Marsden. Why his face is the image of death itself, and his eyes glare; yet my Lady Margaret forsooth! thinks him very handsome, now she is under the influence of the wicked spell; the real Ruthven looked not so when he came to woo the noble fair one; but he says 'tis through his wounds in battle: I think by St. Cuthbert, he has had time enough to get his complexion again, and he eats and drinks voraciously, it makes me sick to see him as I stand in waiting, and no salt – faugh!'

This long soliloquy brought the faithful youth to the door of the baron's prison; he drew the bolts and entered; his Lord was pacing the chamber with unmeasured strides, and beating his forehead, while heavy sighs burst from his aged bosom. He started and stood still on Robert's entrance.

'Friend or foe,' said he. 'Friend,' replied Robert, 'and when I prove otherwise to my most noble master and commander, may I be siezed by the foul fiend and made food for vulture.'

'I am not mad,' said the good old veteran, 'but I think I may say, I am distracted with grief;' 'You are no more mad than I my lord; I do not join in that absurd tale; but hasten and arm yourself? The marriage is to take place almost immediately – let us hasten and prevent it, ere it is too late.'

Lord Ronald was doubly shocked – his suspicions of the Vampire was increased by this obstinate persisting in the nuptials against his command, and the want of tenderness and filial love testified by his daughter. How changed was Margaret! did she choose for her bridal hours those of confinement to her sire – had she not supposed him insane, it is not to be thought she would have suffered him to be thus treated; this then was her season for connubial joys – the sudden insanity of her only surviving parent, he who had so ardently strove not only to fulfil his own duties, but to supply the place as far as possible of the late lady Cassandra, his amiable wife, and he felt there was no sting so keen as a child's ingratitude. The barbed arrow seemed to touch his very vitals, and for the first time in his life the brave Ronald shed tears.

'Take courage, my lord,' said Robert, 'if they dare still to oppose your authority, this trusty falchion, this well tried steel, shall prove if Ruthven is common flesh and blood or no.'

'Moderation! moderation! Robert,' replied the Baron, as he led the way to Lady Margaret's apartment, where he did not arrive one minute too soon – the ceremony was on the point of commencing, and 'tis possible a few of the first words had been pronounced by the priest.

The Baron's entrance caused a universal consternation – the maidens shrieked, and the Vampire began to bluster, but Lord Ronald took prompt measures. He solemnly protested that he was in the full use and exercise of his senses, and charged his daughter, on the penalty of incurring his curse, not to enter into wedlock with Marsden's Earl till he sanctioned it. She did not choose to disobey on such an awful threat, but casting a look of anguish and tenderness on her lover, she burst into tears, and leaning on the arms of her sympathizing maidens, withdrew to her chamber, where throwing herself on a couch, gave way to a full tide of sorrow. 'Cruel father,' she exclaimed! 'ridiculous superstition! I feel I never shall be the bride of my truly adored and adoring Ruthven, so many fatal interruptions seem as if the fates forbid our union – spirits of the storm and air, are ye not too in league against me?'

The Vampire now besought the baron's forgiveness and friendship, attributing his recent behaviour to excess of love, that did not brook delay; he also interceded for the chaplain, whom Lord Ronald was about to dismiss for his presumption, and peace was again restored in the Castle of the Isles.

Wine was called for, and a repast was spread and the Vampire so artfully strove against the suspicions of the Baron, that the prejudices of the latter were nearly done away; and Robert blamed for his credulous folly; yet the false Earl could not obtain from the old nobleman a promise to allow him to wed before the setting of the moon, for Ronald still adhered to that test, nor would abridge, aught of a term that now waxed very short.

The Vampire concealed his chagrin and feigned content; he thought it best to keep a firm footing in the castle, as some chance might still operate in his favour, founding his hopes on the spell he had obtained over Lady Margaret, and the strong affection with which she beheld him, and he scarcely admitted a doubt of success, if he could get the Baron and Robert out of the way; for no one else in the castle had the least doubt of his being the real Earl of Marsden.

The Baron, however, watched with great vigilance, and Robert never stirred from a station he had taken that commanded a view of the door of Lady Margaret's chamber. Time seemed to ride on swift pinions with the Vampire – his fears were stronger than his hopes – he had never been so foiled before in his attempts, and he thought it best to provide against the coming danger, and leave the mistress alone for her allegiance to Robert, persuade her to wed himself, and then sacrifice her to pay his annual demoniac tribute. This would serve two purposes, renew his Vampire-ship, and be a deadly revenge on the interfering Robert, on whom he longed to wreak his diabolical rage.

It seemed rather a difficult achievement to gain the affections of a young and certainly most virtuous maiden, (who was to be married in a few hours to the object of her first choice) from that object, but the Vampire's case grew desperate, and he resolved to try if the charm would operate.

While Robert was watching the lady the Vampire resolved to seize on the more ignoble prize, and he assailed Effie with every alluring temptation. He told the poor girl that he was tired of pursuing the match with Lady Margaret, and abhorred the thoughts of allying himself to such a piece of dotage as the credulous Baron, who was grown superannuated, and only fit to sit amongst the old wives a-spinning, and tell legendary tales of hobgoblins, and water sprites. He said Effie's beauty and innocence had charmed him – that she wanted nothing but dress and rank to be level with her mistress, and that would be hers by marrying Marsden's Earl.

'But I am ignorant, and can neither play music, sing, dance, or do the honours of a table, like Lady Margaret.' This reply pleased the Vampire; it seemed one of a very yielding nature, if she had no scruples but what arose from a fear of her own demerits.

'All these can soon be taught,' said the deceiver. 'I must seek some lady of fallen fortune, but elegant accomplishments, to polish your native gracefulness; she shall be your companion in my absence, and your tutoress, and I will join in the delightful task; therefore that can be no objection.' Effie raised several other difficulties, but all were successfully combated, and the Vampire Earl promised to make the forsaken Robert amends for the loss of his bride by a noble sum and a pretty damsel from off his own estate.

Effie yielded; and though by this act she justly incurred censure and reproach, yet we must do her the justice to remember, that the Vampire had a tongue to charm his victims, and eyes that are described like the fascination of a basilisk; and to have a powerful Earl sighing for her love, might have tempted a higher maid than the simple Effie, the mere child of nature.

Having gained her consent, he hastened to secure his prize; he persuaded her that they must instantly flee, lest the lynx-eyed Robert should grow jealous, and interrupt their promised happiness; he therefore told her, to meet him in an hour, at the end of the long avenue in the castle park, and he would be prepared with a horse to convey her to the next convent, (about five miles distant,) where the priest could join their hands.

That he intended to wed Effie was too true; in that promise lurked no deceit, but the ceremony over, he meant to take her into an adjacent wood, offer up his sacrifice by immolating her with his own hands, and drinking her heart's blood; then seek out some noble form just departed – enter it – and woo Lady Margaret in a new character, and finally triumph over the Baron, for he hated all who opposed him in his designs.

Poor unsuspecting Effie, thy head ran on nothing but the glare of thy expected coronet, and thou felt no pity for thy so lately loved Robert, or thy kind and generous mistress, though both were to be betrayed by this clandestine step.

She was true to her appointment and crossed the park with light steps – the Vampire was in waiting – he assisted her to mount the horse, and then sprung up behind her – The steed bounded off like lightning. In an instant Robert rushed from a copse and cried out for the fugitives to stop, but instead of obeying him the Vampire spurred his horse to quicken him on. The Baron had taken Robert's post to watch the Lady Margaret while the latter made an excursion for air; his gun was loaded, and vengeance nerved the young soldier's arm with so sure an aim that the corporeal part of the Vampire fell mortally wounded to the ground, dragging Effie after it loudly shrieking, and all her new raised love extinguished – for the illusion had vanished, and the image of Robert again filled her virgin heart. Most happily for her future peace the secret of her consenting to the supposed Earl's passion was known to her alone – there had been no witness of that degrading incident so fatal to her integrity; and Robert, believing she was carried off against her will all ended well – she was espoused to her faithful suitor at the appointed time, and made an excellent wife; for her direliction had made her watchful over herself – she often thought of the precipice on which she had stood and trembled. Her beauty long after her marriage gained her admirers, but they were soon dismissed with spirit, and taught to keep at a proper distance, for Effie was now proof against seduction.

But to return to the Vampire. He lay bleeding on the ground, while Robert conveyed Effie to the castle, cautioning her to secrecy as she valued his life, for he knew not what might be the result of this act, if it was indeed Marsden's Earl he had slain. He sought the Baron who was much vexed at the recital, though he acknowledged that Robert had much provocation, and Ruthven's elopement with Effie was an insult on the Lady Margaret not to be borne. The Lord of the Isles and his faithful follower repaired to the spot where the latter had left the treacherous Earl.

'I wonder,' said Robert, as they proceeded hither, and calling to mind the scene in Flanders, 'whether we shall find his lordship there, or whether Beelzebub has given him a second lift.' The Vampire, however, was there, bleeding copiously, but in full possession of his senses. He declared life to be ebbing fast, and that he forgave Robert his death wound; also, he ascribed his carrying off Effie as a mere frolic to alarm her and that he had intended to convey her back in safety to the castle. 'I do not like such jests,' said the indignant Robert, 'and you have paid for an act you had better have left alone.'

The false earl then proceeded to state, on the oath of a dying man, that he was no Vampire. This gave a sad pang both to the baron and Robert, and the former testified his regret at the conduct such suspicions had given rise to. He then demanded of Ruthven if he had any commission to charge him with, and it should be punctually executed.

'Swear it,' exclaimed the Vampire, eagerly.

The baron drew forth his sword and swore on it.

'Give me that topaz ring from off your finger,' said the Vampire; 'let me die with it on, in token of your renewed amity, and allow it to be buried with me.' To this the Lord Ronald most readily consented.

'Next' said the Vampire, drawing it forth from his bosom, where it hung extended by an hair chain, 'take this ring of twisted gold, and cast it into a well that stands on the north side of Fingal's Cave – 'tis a charm given by the mighty Stuffa. I shall thus have a vow performed that will give peace to my soul, and save it from wandering after it has quitted its mortal clay-built tenement. In a few minutes I shall be no more – draw my body aside into the copse, and to-morrow at your return you can seek it, and give me burial; but for the present conceal my death from all you meet: name it not until the ring is in the cave.'

In a few minutes the Vampire seemed to die with a heavy groan, and the afflicted baron and his attendant proceeded to obey the last injunction thus-received, both conscience-stricken at having thus treated Marsden's Earl, and feeling assured, from the manner of his death, that he was a mortal man. They returned to the castle to prepare for their journey to the cave; but mentioned not the decease of Ruthven; and even Effie was imposed on to believe that the wounds, though they had bled much, were but trifling. This gave much comfort to the damsel, as it cleared her Robert of a deed of blood.

The Baron and Robert set out as soon as it dawned, for the cave of Fingal, to perform what they thought an imperious duty, for as such they considered a posthumous request made under such distressing circumstances.

Little did the credulous pair suspect that they were now made the agents of the wicked Vampire, for this is the true story of the magic ring.

The outer part of the Vampire was not subject to disease, and it was invincible to the sword. If they could contrive to have Stuffa's ring flung into the well of the cave of Fingal within twenty-four hours after the death wound it was restored to its vile career for the appointed time, and for that season the malignant spirit hovered round the body.

The good Lord of the Isles and Robert arrived safe there, and with little difficulty found the well, for report had spread its situation far and wide owing to its magic qualities. Lord Ronald cast in the ring – instantaneously a hissing, as if of snakes, followed, but soon all was silent as the grave.

They left the cavern and found themselves in the midst of a pelting storm, and their horses, which they had left tied to a tree, were unloosened and they sought in vain for them. As they continued their search a sweet musical voice was heard by the wanderers.

'Tis Ariel bids you haste away,
'Tis Ariel warns you not to stay;
Hie and stop a horrid scene,

'Tis the fatal *Hallow E'en*,
Haste and save the destined fair
From the treacherous Vampire's snare!'

'Robert,' said the Baron, 'did you hear ought or do my ears deceive me? – again was the verse repeated with this additional stanza –

'Lose not time but quickly see
Whose the triumph is to be,
Margaret must be no more,
Or the Vampire's reign is o'er'

'Tis plane enough, my lord; Ariel, who is always reckoned a benign spirit, warns us – We are deceived – Oh this cursed Vampire! I see it now, he made us tools for his own purpose.'

'Nonsense, my good fellow,' said the Baron, 'it must be some new plot against my peace – a real Vampire, for we left Marsden's Earl quite dead.'

'Oh, he was dead enough in Flanders,' observed Robert, 'but he seems to have as many lives as the Witch of Endor's tabby cat. My mind forbodes horrid things – No harm, however, in getting home quick.'

But they were involved in the intricacies of the forest, and it required both patience and perseverence to find the right track; at length they succeeded, and walked on with rapid strides, for the evening wore away. At this juncture some horsemen overtook them – It was quite dusk and objects scarce discernible.

'Hoy, Holla, my good foresters! can you put us in the way for Baron Ronald's castle; the Lord of the Isles we mean, said the foremost of the caveliers?'

'What want you there?' replied the Baron, (himself) 'let us know ere we guide you, for we are going thither.'

'I am Hildebrand, Lord Gowen's sister's son, sent by my mother to pay my respects and duty to him as becomes a nephew and a godson, nor has he seen me since my infancy.'

'Welcome! Welcome!' exclaimed the Baron, 'son of my beloved Ellen, I am thy uncle, but by some strange accidents, here on foot with one single follower.'

' 'Tis lucky, replied the youth, springing from his steed and embracing the Baron, that we have some led horses in our train.' Lord Ronald and Robert were glad to hear of this seasonable supply, and mounting the noble beasts, set off at full speed.

Hildebrand; as they rode along, was made acquainted with recent events by his worthy uncle – he was struck with terror, and felt much interested for the Lady Margaret; for young Gowen had imbibed from the Countess, (his mother) a strong belief of the existence of Vampires, and he intimated, though respectfully, to his venerable uncle, that he had done wrong by throwing the ring into the well, as by that means it was most probable, the wicked sprite had acquired reanimation.

Again the storm arose and served to retard their progress, for the steeds affrighted at the vivid and incessant lighting, could with difficulty be got forward. At length they arrived at the copse, and Robert with two of Earl Gowen's serving men dismounted to seek for the body, but it was not there. 'Just as I thought to find it,' said the former, 'beshrew me it is an industrious sprite; but the moon will soon set,' and as the benign Ariel sang –

> 'Let's haste and save the destin'd fair
> From the treacherous Vampire's snare.'

They spurred their horses, and the storm having made a temporary stop they were soon across the park. Music was sounding – they could distinguish the harper's strain – the great hall was lighted up most brilliantly – a sumptuous altar had been erected at one end – and for the third time, the marriage ceremony was about to begin, when the Baron, Lord Gowen and Robert rushed in and secured the intended bride, who fainted immediately, for in the person of her noble cousin she beheld the form shewn her by Una and Ariel in the cave of Fingal, and the Vampire's charm vanished away like snow before the meridian sun.

The Vampire seemed armed with supernatural strength – he resisted all their efforts to subdue him – and their swords made no impression – he struggled hard to bear away the Lady Margaret from the midst of her protectors, and the amazing efforts of the Vampire spread horror and alarm, for that he was an evil sprite no one now doubted. He had returned to the castle that evening, and said he came with the Baron's consent, (who had undertaken a sudden journey) to wed the Lady Margaret, and had brought her father's ring as a token. All was now bustle, preparation and joy, till the unexpected entrance of the Lord of the Isles and his companions, and had it not been for the providence of Gowen seeking the castle that night, the fiend would have triumphed, for they could not have got home on foot time enough to save her.

But the fiend was not to be overpowered – he jumped on the temporary altar sword in hand (after having wounded and bit with his teeth several of the domestics) insisting he would yet have his bride. In an instant the scene changed – the moon set – the thunder rolled over the castle, and the bolt fell on the Vampire – he rolled lifeless upon the floor, and after a terrific yell, melted into air, incorporeal and invisible to every eye. Thus ended the wicked sprite.

Some months after this event Margaret was happily united to Earl Gowen, with whom she led a happy life till they both sunk into the grave, venerable with age, making good the prediction of the spirits of the cave of Fingal –

'Ne'er but once was she to wed,
Or have a second bridal bed.'

www.ingramcontent.com/pod-product-compliance
Lightning Source LLC
Chambersburg PA
CBHW030532260626
47157CB00005B/1999